The legend of
ROBIN HOOD

BARNES & NOBLE BOOKS
NEW YORK

THE STORY OF ROBIN HOOD

That a man called Robin Hood, an elusive outlaw and infallible archer, ever existed has never quite been confirmed. Various historians have done studies and research, some have traced his genealogical tree, and have even established a date of death, 18 November 1247; in truth, however, nothing could really be ascertained, and his character has remained in shadow. And yet, few figures have been as celebrated as he has, nor have generated as much interest, admiration, and emotion. So many books have been written on Robin Hood that it is impossible to count them; at various times films have been made, all successful; and in fact the most recent film based on the life of Robin Hood was seen worldwide.

Some thought that it would no longer be possible to interest the public in adventures that, more or less, everyone already knows; and, instead, millions of spectators of all ages showed their interest. What is even more interesting is that no one has ever thought (as has happened in other cases) of presenting his character in a negative light.

Possibly he never existed except in legend and people's imaginations; but for centuries he has been the protagonist of daring adventures, narrated first by minstrels, then by poets, then by novelists. Robin Hood continues to inspire people.

Who has not dreamed of being as agile as he with bow and arrow, or as knowledgeable about the forest, or as loyal and courageous? Who hasn't wished to have friends like he has, such as Little John, Friar Tuck, and all the other merry companions of Sherwood Forest?

Robin Hood's fame and glory have been passed down from generation to generation, and his story (or perhaps, his legend) has slowly been enriched with new episodes, because every generation wanted to be just a little like him: rebellious, proud, fighting for justice for the poor against the powerful and wealthy. This is why Robin Hood is a hero on whom the sun never sets.

THE CASTLE
OF HUNTINGDON

In the year 1189, upon the death of King Henry II, Prince Richard took the throne of England. He was called, for his courage, Richard the Lion-Hearted. Chivalrous, bold, and adventurous, when he found out that the King of France, Philip Augustus, and the Emperor of Germany, Frederick the Red-Beard, were preparing to leave for a crusade—a war that would hunt down the Muslims from Palestine and liberate the Sepulchre of Jesus—he decided to go with them.

He told his younger brother, "John, you will reign over England during my absence. Try to be fair and generous, and do everything you can to make the Normans and Saxons become a united people."

Prince John kissed his hand, responding, "I will hold the crown until your return, and I will do as you tell me."

Richard the Lion-Hearted then left, leading his most valiant soldiers, but his departure caused a great deal of worry.

England, in fact, was inhabited by two populations of different origins: the Normans and the Saxons.

The latter were the ancient inhabitants of the country and they had reigned over it until it was invaded and conquered by the Normans.

Many years had passed since then, but the conflict between the conquerors and the conquered was still very much alive.

The Norman nobles were lords of castles and cities, from which they banished the Saxons, who were often treated harshly and with contempt.

King Richard, who was of Norman ancestry, had thought a great deal about what he could do to bring peace and harmony.

"We must not be two rival populations," he proclaimed, "but a united people.

6

We must no longer be Normans and Saxons, but only English."

This is why his departure caused consternation, especially among the Saxons, who knew well how little interest and consideration Prince John had for them.

"When King Richard is far away," they said, "John will persecute us." They were right.

After several years had passed and King Richard had still not returned from the Holy Land (it was rumored that he had been killed in battle or taken prisoner), Prince John began to act as if he were king. He took every opportunity to favor his Norman friends over the Saxons, who were pushed from other cities and castles. Among these, was the castle of Huntingdon, which stood not far from the city of Nottingham.

Prince John hired one of his friends, who was as greedy, false, and cruel as he was, to govern this city with the title of sheriff.

One of the sheriff's first acts was to take over the castle of Huntingdon and its lands.

The castle was inhabited by a Saxon noble count, who defended himself with his faithful as long as he could; when he finally realized that he had no other choice, he had his wife and young son Robert leave through a secret little door.

"Run, save yourself and our son, my wife," he said, "and I will stay to face my destiny."

"Let me stay by your side, Father!" said his son. "No. Save yourself and protect your mother," said his father. The boy lowered his head. The count

was put in Nottingham prison, which he never left again; a sad end also awaited his wife, who died of fever some time later. Young Robert, alone, with no relatives, no home, no money, and hunted by the Sheriff of Nottingham, had no other option but to hide himself away in Sherwood Forest.

7

ROBERT BECOMES ROBIN HOOD

Sherwood Forest was one of the largest and most intricate in all of England. It was crossed by a winding road that ran from Sheffield to Nottingham, and contained many footpaths. Only he who knew them well could follow them, because it was very easy to lose one's way and become a prisoner in the forest. There were some woodsmen's and woodcutters' cottages near the forest. Robert went and knocked on the door of one of these and to the man who opened it, he said, "In the name of God, give me something to eat or I will die of hunger."

The woodsman asked, "Who are you? Are you a Saxon or a Norman?" Fearing that he would be taken to the Sheriff of Nottingham, and thus not wanting to use his real name, Robert responded, "My name is Robin Hood. I am poor, therefore I am Saxon, and if you will feed me I can do some work for you." The woodsman thought for a moment, then said, "All right, take this," and he gave the boy an ax, adding, "follow me, and maybe today you will have something to eat."

Robin obeyed, and for the rest of the day he chopped wood. He did it so well that in the evening he was invited to sit down to eat with the woodsman. Robin was so hungry that he ate with gusto, and then he said to the woodsman's wife, "You are a very good cook."

"The cook," she said, "is actually my niece, Marian. Here she comes now."

A girl with long red braids, green eyes, and a beautiful countenance appeared, carrying a bucket of water. She was so beautiful that Robin was enchanted looking at her, and he said, "If you want, and if every day you will give me something to eat, I will stay here and work for you."

"Fine," responded the woodsman. And he added, "Go on, Marian and Robin, shake hands." So the young people did, but they both blushed and said nothing. Thus, Robert of Huntingdon became Robin Hood, and he stayed at the woodsman's cottage, quickly learning the forest and its most secret corners. He also learned to shoot with a bow and arrow, and he showed such ability that he surprised everyone. There wasn't a target he couldn't hit. At the very first competition Robin participated in, he tied with old Hugo, who was considered the best archer in the county.

Hugo remarked, "It seems as if you were born with a bow in your hands, my boy."

Once, while he was practicing archery with Marian, she said to him, "Robin, by now you could get all the game you want—except the deer, of course."

"And why shouldn't I shoot the deer?"

"Don't you know? They belong to the king, and if the sheriff's men find you hunting one, then they will take you to Nottingham."

"And what happens in Nottingham?"

"The sheriff has you hanged, that's what happens!"

"Really?" exclaimed the young man.

"He is a ruthless man, like Prince John. Oh, I wish our good King Richard would come back soon!"

THE OUTLAWS OF SHERWOOD

Robin lived with the woodsman's family for several years, and he might have stayed there forever, if one day several gamekeepers in the sheriff's service had not come to the little cottage in the forest.

Arrogant and bullying, they entered noisily, and demanded food and drink. "Hurry up, you miserable Saxons!" one of them said. "You, old man, prepare some meat, and a lot of it. You women, bring us some wine. And you, young Saxon, sing a song for us."

"I don't know how to sing," said Robin, "I don't know any songs."

"I'll teach you one," exclaimed another gamekeeper, "it is called, 'The Song of the Count of Huntingdon'."

At this name, which he had tried to forget for many years, Robin felt a burning inside himself and he replied, "How does the song go?"

Laughing scornfully, the other began, "In a handsome castle, there lived a count, who was ready to run—" He couldn't continue, because Robin was on top of him and with two well-placed punches, he knocked him to the floor. When they overcame their surprise, the other gamekeepers tried to catch him, but they, too, fell under Robin's furious fists.

"Oh, what have you done, Robin?" exclaimed the woodsman. "Now they will catch you and you will be hanged in Nottingham Square!"

"Where I will go they will never catch me!" replied the young man and he took his bow and arrows and said, "Thank you for everything you have done for me—I will pay you back somehow. Good-bye!" He ran out of the cottage and disappeared into the trees.

In Sherwood Forest, there was not only wild game. Various men were also hidden there; all Saxons, bandits and fugitives from their cities.

Afraid of being caught by the sheriff's men, they were constantly on guard. They were, therefore, quickly aware of Robin's presence and jumping from the trees, they surrounded him with their weapons raised.

"Who are you? What are you doing here?" they asked.

Robin told them his story, and they then responded, "If you are an enemy of the Normans, you are welcome here, Robin Hood. You will take part in our affairs!"

"And what might they be?"

"The hunting of royal deer!" replied a young man who seemed to be the leader and who called himself Scarlet, "And also travelers who cross the forest. We don't hurt them, we don't take their lives: we limit ourselves to taking their money!"

Everyone laughed, but Robin Hood exclaimed, "No. I will not join a band of robbers. Good-bye!"

Now everyone was silent, and Scarlet murmured, "But, Robin Hood, we have to live, that's why we rob the travelers."

"One needs little money to live in the forest," said Robin. "What do you do with the money you get? I'll tell you what you should do with it: give it to the poor."

"Give it to the poor?" repeated the bandits. "Yes. You know very well that in the villages around you there are many families reduced to misery by the sheriff. If you help these poor people, they will love you; when King Richard returns to England, he will pardon all of you." Scarlet thought, and said, "Well, all right, Robin Hood, we will do as you say. We are at your command!"

LUNCH UNDER THE OAK TREE

From that time on, in all of England, people began to hear of the outlaws of Sherwood. Extremely able archers, they kept vigil from the trees on the road and footpaths that crossed the forest, and when they saw someone rich passing by, they stripped him of his money.

The merchants who drove their caravans, the horsemen with their escorts of pages and squires, abbots and their attendants, found themselves suddenly surrounded by men wearing caps each adorned with a long pheasant's feather, and with bows ready in hand. The outlaws seemed to come out of nowhere. They leapt from branches, came out of bushes, and jumped out of holes dug in the ground. The bold young man who led them would come forward and say, "Sir, may I ask where you are going?"

"I am going to Nottingham for business," the merchants or gentlemen would say. Others would respond, "I am going to Sheffield to visit a friend."

"Would you like to eat with us?" Robin Hood would ask. Generally the response was yes, and those invited were led to a clearing where, under an old oak tree, a very long table would be set. They would eat roast meat, rabbit pie, birds on the spit, and drink good wine or clear spring water.

At the end, Robin Hood would ask, "Sir, have you eaten well?"

"Yes, certainly, certainly!"

"I am glad. But, you see, to make a rich Norman like yourself happy, we poor Saxons have had to sacrifice for a long time; therefore, I must ask you to pay for your meal."

"Of course, my dear friend, he who eats must pay!"

"Yes, but the fact is, sir, that you will have to pay for us as well. You know we cannot afford such rich meals."

Usually, the guests understood, paid as much as they were asked, and they were allowed to go. Those who refused to pay, however, had their pockets and purses emptied. The same happened to those who did not accept the invitation to dine.

From the money they got this way, Robin Hood and his companions kept what they absolutely needed; the rest was distributed to the poor, and to the families of prisoners of the Sheriff of Nottingham.

These families blessed the outlaws of Sherwood, and Robin Hood's enterprises began to be told throughout England. The Sheriff of Nottingham was furious; he had never been defied like this.

He sent his men into the forest many times, with the orders to take Robin Hood, dead or alive. Sometimes, the men never came back, sometimes they returned battered and frightened, announcing, "Robin Hood said that he will come to Nottingham!"

"He will never dare to come here!" thought the sheriff. But one day while feasting with his guests he was interrupted. An arrow came whizzing through the window and planted itself threateningly in the table. It was one of Robin Hood's arrows.

LITTLE JOHN

One spring morning, after having hunted a royal deer, Robin was returning toward the Great Oak. Whistling happily, he came upon a river, and was about to step onto its wooden bridge—when he stopped. On the bridge, was a large, fat man, who held a long pole and who did not seem to want to move and let Robin pass by. Robin said to him, "Friend, this bridge is too narrow for both of us. It's better if you decide: forward or backward."

"And why," asked the man, who had a big blond beard, "should I decide?"
"Because either way you get off the bridge and I can pass."
"Oh yes? And what if I do not want to let you pass?"
In a moment Robin had disposed of the deer that he had had on his shoulders, raised his bow, and cocked an arrow. "Get off!" he ordered.
The man spread his arms, "Oh no, that's not fair. You have a bow, I have

14

only a pole. How can I defend myself?" Robin threw down his bow and cut a branch from a tree. "We'll fight with equal weapons, fair enough?"

"Fair enough!" The two began battle on the little bridge with their long poles, which both knew how to maneuver very well, crossing them from low to high, sparring, and hitting again and again.

The sound of the poles was so loud it resonated throughout the silent forest. The outlaws seated around the oak tree heard it and ran toward the point from whence it came.

Meanwhile, the duel continued until Robin hit his adversary so hard that he fell into the water with a great splash.

"Had enough?" asked Robin.

The man stood up, dripping, and answered, "No, not yet!" then struck Robin so hard that he tumbled right into the river.

Robin Hood got up and the two once again faced one another. Seeing themselves so completely drenched, they began to laugh, and Robin said, "The bridge is no longer very useful for crossing the river. You are truly good with that pole, my friend, but what are you doing in the forest?"

"You are good, too. What am I doing? I am looking for Robin Hood."

"And why are you looking for him?" asked Robin suspiciously. "Has the Sheriff of Nottingham sent you here, perhaps?"

"What do you mean? I am only looking for him because I want to join his band of outlaws!"

"If that is why, then you have found him. I am Robin Hood!"

"You?" exclaimed the man. "I have hit Robin Hood, then?"

"Yes, but now we are friends," and Robin raised his right hand, saying, "you are one of us, now. What's your name?"

"I am called John Little," said the large man. Robin began to laugh, "John Little? No, from now on you will be Little John!" Just then, his forest companions arrived. "What was all that noise?" asked Scarlet.

"A fair duel that ended in a tie. But I must tell you that we have gained something. We now have a new friend—and his name is Little John!"

ALAN DALE'S WOES

It was sunset. The sun descended red among the clouds, and it streaked them with its golden rays. Robin and Little John were heading down a path, chatting. Robin asked, "Tell me, Little John, what made you decide to come to the forest?"

"Well, I was tired of living as a servant. I was working in a mill, in the village of Limby, and the owner never lost an occasion to mortify and humiliate me every day. I couldn't stand his bullying anymore, so—" Little John interrupted himself and said, "Listen. What's that noise?"

Robin Hood cocked his ear and murmured, "That's not a noise, Little John. It's the sound of a harp. It's very melancholy, don't you think?"

A little while later, guided by the sound, the two reached a clearing and saw, sitting under a tree, a young man dressed in red, who was singing and accompanying himself on the harp, and he did not stop playing as he watched the two outlaws come closer. Robin Hood asked him, "Who are you? What's your name?"

"I am an unhappy man," was the answer, "and my name is Alan Dale."

"And why do you play in the forest, where no one can hear you?"

"I do not play to be heard by others, I play for myself, to console my pain and my unhappiness."

"And why are you unhappy?"

Getting up and with a profound sigh, Alan Dale responded, "Because I cannot marry the maiden whom I love and who loves me." Perplexed, Little John asked, "Why can't you get married?"

The young man sadly shook his head and said, "My love's parents do not want her to marry a man as poor as I. Thus, they have promised their daughter to a rich merchant. The wedding will take place tomorrow at the church in Limby. I am sure you can understand, then, why I am hidden away here, and why I sing these sad love songs. Well, friends, good-bye." And the young man began to walk away.

Robin whispered, "Little John, we must do something."

"Robin, one should never get involved in affairs of love, maidens, and weddings."

"Yes, but let's at least go console Alan, come on." They set off, and once again found the young man, who was sitting down and crying, contemplating a wild rose. Robin asked him, "What about your maiden?"

"She will die of pain. I will die too, and then it will be over."

"Amen!" exclaimed Little John, "Let's go, Robin."

"No, wait. Tell me, who is the promised husband?"

"William of Limby, an old and very arrogant Norman."

"Why, it's that dishonest boss of mine!" exclaimed Little John. "Oh, Robin, we must do something!"

"But you just said that one should never meddle in affairs of love, maidens, and weddings!"

"Well, yes, but . . . but, heck, this is something else! Alan and his maiden are in love, and we must help them!"

Robin Hood then said, "Calm yourself, Alan. There will be a wedding in the church in Limby, yes. But not the one everyone is expecting."

A MERRY WEDDING

The next morning, a small crowd awaited the arrival of the betrothed in front of the church.

The parish priest stood in the church square surrounded by altar boys holding candles, as the bell rang musically. But there was no air of festivity. Everyone in Limby knew that what they were about to celebrate was not a marriage of love, and that the bride, the sweet Edith, had cried all night.

No one felt much sympathy for the husband-to-be, a greedy and miserly merchant. William of Limby arrived first, pompous and potbellied, in a red suit with gold fringe. There were many rich Normans with him. He passed among the people, ordering, "Make way, make way! Hey, you, priest!" He then asked, "Where is my bride? Late, huh? Well, when she is my wife I'll teach her better manners! And you, who are you?"

This last question was aimed at a man in a tattered shawl and a cap with a feather in it. The man answered, "I am a harp player." And thus saying, he produced a harp. "If you want, I will play for you and make your wedding a joyful occasion."

"Hmm. And so how much do you want, to play?"

"Nothing. I will do it without asking you for a penny."

"In that case, you can play. Ah, finally, here is my bride!"

Edith, in fact, had appeared, accompanied by her mother and father. The young woman was sad and appeared disconsolate.

William of Limby took her gruffly by the arm, saying, "Come on, hurry up, my business is waiting. You, play your harp!"

Robin Hood (who was in disguise) replied, "I will play my trumpet, instead!" Amid the general stupor he pulled out a trumpet and blew into it hard. The call echoed all over, and from the nearby forest men came out with arms ready, surrounding the priest, betrothed, and wedding guests. Frightened, William of Limby shouted, "What is the meaning of this? I beg you, don't hurt me!"

Robin Hood said, "No one will be hurt. Everyone into the church; follow me. You, priest, please stand next to me." Scared, all of the guests obeyed. Robin walked to the altar and said, "A wedding must be celebrated, and it will be celebrated. Will the bride please come forward!"

Trembling, Edith went to the altar, and Robin continued, "Now, you, William of Limby!"

Staggering, the merchant made his way to stand by the maiden.

"And now, Alan Dale, will you please come forward!"

Stupefied, everyone whispered among themselves as Alan entered the church and glided up to the altar.

Robin Hood again continued, "Go on, priest, ask the maiden whom she wants to marry, to whom she will say 'I do'." Stunned, the priest asked, "Edith, do you want to marry this man, William of Limby?"

"No!" answered the maiden.

The priest then asked, "Edith, do you want to marry this man, Alan Dale?"

"Yes! A thousand times, yes!"

"I then declare you man and wife!"

"Hurrah!" shouted Robin. "Hurrah!"
echoed his men, and they set off for the
forest. Recovering from the shock,
William of Limby shouted, "I will get
you! I will denounce you to the sheriff!
Who are you, you, who dared to do
this?" "I am Robin Hood!"

A REWARD FOR ROBIN HOOD

The news of Robin Hood's deeds finally reached Prince John, and they filled him with indignation and worry.

To the sheriff, who received him with every honor in his castle, he said, annoyed, "I greatly appreciate these banquets, this applause, and this lavishly set table, but I would appreciate the capture of Robin Hood much more. Why are you waiting to catch him?"

Sighing with frustration, the sheriff said, "It is not easy to catch a man like Robin Hood, Your Highness. I have sent many of my good men into the forest, but always in vain."

"Well, send some more. I do not want the people to think that there is a revolt going on against me. Look—" and thus saying, Prince John deposited a leather pouch on the table, "here are one hundred gold coins that the Norman merchants brought me. Put up posters, send your men all over the region, advertise that he who captures Robin Hood or who tells us how to capture him will have these one hundred gold coins as a reward!"

So the sheriff did, and, naturally, there were several people who in hope of earning that sum, ventured into

Sherwood Forest in search of the infamous Robin Hood.

He was on guard more than ever: every woodsman, every hunter could be an enemy; every traveler could also be one. Thick bands of armed men kept watch over the traffic on the road and the main footpaths; soldiers on horseback traveled without rest through the forest, from which it had by now become impossible to exit.

Two poor hunters were arrested as outlaws and taken to Nottingham where, despite their desperate pleas, the sheriff had them hanged from gallows he had erected in the main square. Their bodies were left hanging from the gallows for two days, and the people looked at them dumbstruck and scared.

More than once, the sheriff's soldiers penetrated the forest and there were some skirmishes.

The outlaws, keeping themselves hidden in the trees, bombarded the enemy with arrows, and they were always the better fighters, but in one encounter, Robin himself was wounded in a sword fight, and he was carried, unconscious, to the Great Oak.

FRIAR TUCK

Robin's wound was not very serious, but it required care that none of the merry outlaws of Sherwood could provide. So Alan Dale said, "I've heard tell that at Fountain Abbey there is a friar who is very able in medicine. Let's take Robin to him, and he will take care of him."

Scarlet answered, "No, Robin is too weak to endure a journey, even on a stretcher."

"I have an idea!" exclaimed Little John. "If we cannot take Robin to the friar, let's bring the friar to Robin. What do you say?"

Everyone liked the idea, and the same day Scarlet, Alan, and Little John set off for Fountain Abbey. After two days of walking they arrived.

The abbey stood over a river with shallow and very clear water, and right on the banks of the little river was a small, round friar, intent on rinsing some linens.

Upon hearing the footfalls of the three approaching, he turned his red face and said, "Peace to you, strangers."

"Peace to you, friar," answered Little John. "Is this Fountain Abbey? I have been told that there is a friar here who is good at curing wounds, is this true?" The friar made a face and said, "It is true. But none of you seems wounded."

"In fact, we ask for our friend, and he is why we are here. Please, friar, take us to your brother the doctor."

"How was your friend wounded?" asked the friar.

"It was during a hunt . . . an arrow hit him by accident."

The fat friar asked again, "And where did this happen?"

Then Scarlet exclaimed, "Friar, you ask too many questions. Friends, let's leave this gossip and go to the abbey!" and he set off, beginning to cross the river.

Alan and Little John started to follow him, when the friar shouted, "Where are you going? . . . I am the one you're looking for. I am Friar Tuck, the fix-it-all."

"Are you the doctor?" asked a surprised Little John.

Scarlet said, "And why didn't you tell us right away?"

And Alan added, "Then, come with us." Friar Tuck rebuked, "Me? Not even for a song. I want to know the truth. You have told me only lies."

"If you do not come with us of your own free will," muttered Little John, "you will go by our will."

Crossing his arms, the friar asked, "Oh, yes? And how?"

The three put their hands on their swords, but before they could grab them, Friar Tuck jumped on them, hitting Scarlet with a punch, Alan with another, and Little John with a head-butt in the stomach. Within a minute, the three found themselves sitting in the water, stupefied and bruised. Threateningly, the friar said, "You know that I do nothing against God's will or my own."

"Yes, but this involves curing a wound," said Little John.

"I do not cure any wound, if I am forced to do it!" replied the friar, and added, "Unless it's for Robin Hood!"

The three, still seated in the water, exchanged glances and Little John exclaimed, "Friar Tuck, it is for Robin."

"Robin Hood?" exclaimed the friar. "And why didn't you tell me right away? Wait for me, I'll get my bag and be right with you!"

AN UNEXPECTED VISITOR

After the friar had put some ointment on the outlaw's wound, and bandaged it, Robin Hood got better quickly.

"Friar Tuck," he said, while his bandage was being taken off, "we're very sorry to see you return to the abbey. We all like you very much here, and we will miss you."

"I will miss you, too," answered Friar Tuck, "because I have felt better here in the forest with you than in the abbey with my brothers—" he paused, because an outlaw had arrived, running, who announced, "Robin, a stranger is coming in this direction!"

"A spy for the sheriff?"

"Probably. Shall we kill him?"

"No. I need news. I'll deal with him. You stay here." And saying thus, Robin Hood hurried along a path, without listening to Friar Tuck, who shouted to him, "Don't use force, Robin!"

Shortly, Robin caught sight of the intruder. He was thin and agile, had his head and face hidden by a large hat, and walked with confidence, as if he knew the forest well. He was not armed, but he carried only a long pole. The outlaw waited a moment, then throwing his hood over his head, he stepped out of the bushes and said, "Stop where you are, friend, and tell me where you are going."

"Why should I tell you?" answered a young and proud voice.

"Because I say so," replied Robin and he raised the pole he had with him, "and if you do not speak up, you will taste this!"

Preparing for a fight, the stranger replied, "Go to it, then!"

If Robin Hood had listened to Friar Tuck's recommendations, he would not have been hit.

He realized right away that he was too weak to do battle, and he realized it when his adversary's pole hit him, and he felt his knee buckle. "You are good and you are smooth!" Robin said. "Too bad you are a spy!"

"A spy?" responded the youth. "Now I'll teach you to respect me!" And he landed two or three more hard blows.

Robin, as much as he felt weak and in pain, went into counterattack, landing a blow that sent his adversary's legs out from under him, and making his large hat fly off his head. A cascade of long red hair flowed out. Robin shouted, "Marian!"

Yes, it was Marian, who, unable to stand Robin's absence any longer, had come into the forest to find him.

The two embraced, and a little while later they arrived under the Great Oak holding hands, where Robin said, "Before leaving, Tuck, you must do me a service."

"What might that be?"

"You must celebrate my wedding to Marian, the most beautiful maiden in all of England!"

"Hurrah!" everyone shouted.

THE SHERIFF'S TRAP

The Sheriff of Nottingham became angrier and angrier that nothing could be done against the outlaws of Sherwood. In his castle one day, reflecting on what had happened and looking at the arrow that Robin had sent him, he had an idea.

He jumped up, and the dark Sir Maddock, his adviser, asked him, "What's the matter, sir? Why the satisfied expression?"

"An idea has come to me, Maddock. We might have Robin Hood in our hands!"

"What? Have you found a way to capture him?"

"Yes. He is a great archer, everyone knows that. And everyone knows that archers love competition ... Maddock, listen up!"

The sheriff laid out his plan.

The next day, everyone knew that a grand tournament would be held in Nottingham. There would be a challenge of horsemen, fencing, and, finally, an archery competition. The winner would receive a magnificent hunting bugle finished in pure gold.

A big ring was set up in the open space east of the city and hurdles and pavilions began to be erected.

The organizers spread the word all over. Long lines of curious people and merchants headed toward Nottingham. Naturally, the news reached the outlaws' camp, under the Great Oak, and Robin Hood muttered, "An archery contest ... I would definitely like to participate."

"Oh, Robin," responded the beautiful Marian, "you don't want to go to Nottingham, the sheriff's den."

"I certainly won't go," said Little John, "because they would recognize my face.

But Robin could go. No one knows what he looks like."

"And then, he would certainly be the winner," observed Alan.

It was discussed, and finally Robin decided to go to Nottingham to compete. "But naturally, I won't go in this outfit. I will dress as a gamekeeper. Never fear. I will return victorious and we'll have a grand party!"

Honest as he was, he could not imagine that the competition could be a trap engineered for his capture.

The tournament began a few days later. In front of the stand where ladies and gentlemen were seated, the horsemen faced each other in individual duels. Then, they fenced with blunt weapons, cropped lances, and dull swords. The enthusiasm and applause grew when the heralds announced that the archery contest would begin.

The sheriff, who was sitting in the center of the stand, held up the precious bugle offered as a prize for the contestants.

Then he muttered, "My men have surrounded the field. Robin Hood will not escape."

ROBIN HOOD'S CAPTURE

Trumpet blares, shouts, and applause greeted the twenty archers who were preparing for the competition.

They were almost all gamekeepers who worked for various gentlemen of the region. Old and young, they were all equally daring, and they had large bows and quivers full of arrows. When they were called forward for the first shots, Maddock murmured, "I wonder which one is Robin?"

"Do you think he came?" the sheriff asked in a whisper.

"You can be sure of it!"

Robin was, in fact, among the competitors, and he was dressed as one of the Count of Sambury's gamekeepers. Perfectly calm and sure of himself, Robin was able to think of nothing but the contest ahead.

They began with the qualifying shots, at the end of which, of twenty competitors only five remained; then they continued with targets that were farther and farther away, until only two archers were left.

"The winner," shouted a herald, "will be one of these two valiant men: Hubert, a gamekeeper for the Count of Malvoisin, and Locksley, a gamekeeper for the Count of Sambury!"

The two stepped forward and launched their arrows toward the target, first seventy meters away, then eighty, and finally ninety. That was the maximum distance.

The adversaries were tied. The last shot would indicate the winner.

There was a profound silence as Hubert cocked his arrow and pulled back on the bow. After having carefully eyed the target, the gamekeeper for the Count of Malvoisin let his arrow fly: the arrow planted itself exactly in the center of the target.

A hurricane of applause rose up and someone shouted, "Locksley, you can't do better than that!"

Locksley (for this was the name with which Robin Hood had entered the contest) responded, "We shall see. I can't hit the center of the target, but I can hit Hubert's arrow." And thus saying, he raised his bow, took a quick glance, and let the arrow sail. There was a great silence.

The arrow had driven itself right into Hubert's arrow. He had hit the center of the center! There were shouts, hurrahs, and applause.

Hubert raised his arms in a sign of surrender and exclaimed, "I declare myself beaten! Locksley, you are not a man, you are a devil!"

Robin Hood smiled, and after a little while he went to the judges to receive his prize from the hands of the most beautiful woman in Nottingham.

He did not realize that, hidden in the crowd, the sheriff's men were slowly moving forward.

The sheriff was agitated. "Maddock," he growled, "let's get him in our possession. Go ahead and have him arrested, now!"

"Not yet, sir, there is too much confusion. We'll get him when he is about to leave the grounds."

The bugle was truly magnificent. Robin Hood raised it for the crowd to see, and there was another round of applause. The young man slung his bow over his shoulder and started off. He had just left the field when he found himself in front of Maddock, who said, "Are you going already, Locksley, my boy?"

"Yes, sir. I am going back to my boss, the Count of Sambury," responded Robin, still not suspecting that anything was amiss.

"You don't want to stay a little longer?"

"I would like to, but—" Robin could not finish as ten men jumped on him. He could do nothing to defend himself, and in an instant he found himself tied up tightly. He heard the mocking voice of Maddock say, "I think instead that you will stay quite awhile in Nottingham, Robin Hood!"

FRIAR TUCK'S DARING

Before the sun had set, the news of Robin Hood's capture had reached the Great Oak.

"Silence!" said Friar Tuck finally. "I have an idea. I'll take care of Robin! Don't ask me what I want to do. If I make a mistake, you can hang me from this oak tree." Tuck mounted his horse and galloped at full speed all the way to Nottingham, all the while pulling a second horse behind him. It was dawn when he finally tied the beasts to a tree in the forest, and presented himself at the city's gates.

Lowering his lance, the sentry exclaimed, "Halt, there! No one can pass, by orders of the sheriff!"

"How can you threaten a friar like this?" replied Tuck. "As for the sheriff, it is to him that I am headed. Get out of the way!"

The confused sentry moved out of the way, and Tuck continued along the almost empty streets of Nottingham to the castle, and knocked on the door. To the guard who opened the spy window, he said, "Let me in, I must speak to the sheriff."

The guard answered, "The sheriff is sleeping, and it is forbidden to wake him up."

"My time is more precious than the sheriff's sleep! Come on, open up. I must go to comfort someone condemned to death."

The guard protested, and said that it

was impossible, but Friar Tuck raised his voice and threatened so much, that the guard finally obeyed. When he reached the jail, the friar asked, "Where is the outlaw's cell?"

"It is that one, but I'm afraid I cannot open the door."

"In fact, you will close it as soon as I am inside, and reopen it only to let me out again." Reassured, the guard opened the door and closed it again immediately. In a loud voice the friar said, "Robin Hood, you are about to die: do you want to make a confession?" Robin recognized his friend immediately, and said, "Yes, father! I will kneel down in front of you!" Under the careful watch of the guard, Friar Tuck spoke as if accepting Robin Hood's confession, while he whispered the plan.

When he was done, he turned to the guard and said, "We are finished. Open up, guard!"

The guard opened the door. Closing it again, he said, "Ha ha, Robin Hood! Now you will be able to sleep an eternal sleep!"

"You, instead," hissed Friar Tuck, who was behind him, "will sleep a briefer sleep!" He hit the guard over the head with a pole. While the guard crumpled to the ground, the friar opened the door and ordered, "Hurry up, Robin!"

FLIGHT FROM NOTTINGHAM

A while later, when the sun had already risen, Tuck presented himself once again at the gates where he had entered the city.

One of the sheriff's guards accompanied him, with a lance in one hand. The friar said to the sentry, "You can open, friend. My work is already done. And you," he added, turning to the guard, "can return to the castle."

"I'm sorry," replied the guard harshly, "the sheriff ordered me to escort you to your horse and I must obey!"

"I am a friar! I do not want to be escorted like a criminal!"

"You tell him, friend, that orders are orders!" said the guard to the sentry, who answered gravely, "That's right. Don't make such a fuss, friar, and let my companion do his job."

Sighing, Friar Tuck left Nottingham, followed by Robin Hood who (as readers will have understood by now) had worn the castle guard's uniform. The two quickly reached the horses. A minute later they were galloping, laughing, to the heart of Sherwood. Meanwhile, the sheriff awakened and had his faithful Maddock summoned. "Are the gallows ready?" he asked him.

"Yes. A nice gallows with a nice noose. There's a problem, though."

"Which would be?"

"Rumor is," said Maddock, "that the people do not want to come to the square. In fact, they do not want to see Robin Hood die."

The sheriff smiled cruelly and said, "I will order all of Nottingham to assist in the hanging of Robin Hood. And meanwhile, Maddock, let's go chat with our captured bandit."

The two went down into the prison. Reaching the prison guard they asked, "Everything all right?"

"Just fine. I looked at the bandit through the window. He is sleeping."

"Ha!" sneered the sheriff, "within an hour he will sleep even more. Come on, open up." The prison guard obeyed, and the sheriff and Sir Maddock entered the cell. Rolling the prone man on the floor over with a kick, Maddock said, "Wake up, Robin Hood,

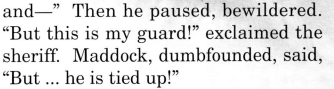

and—" Then he paused, bewildered. "But this is my guard!" exclaimed the sheriff. Maddock, dumbfounded, said, "But ... he is tied up!"

"And Robin Hood! Where is Robin Hood?" shouted the sheriff. "He has escaped!" The two stumbled out of the cell and sounded a general alarm. Maddock, on horseback, toured the gates, ordering each one barred. When he asked who entered and exited, the sentry answered, "From here, sir,

a good friar came through. After a little while, he left again; he was escorted by a castle guard. Now that I think of it, that guard hasn't come back yet—"

"And he'll never come back!" shouted Maddock, lashing out at him with a blow. "That guard was Robin Hood, you fool!"

Robin reached the Great Oak by evening, where the beautiful Marian, crying with joy, ran to embrace him, and a great party began.

THE FOUR ARCHERS

It was winter.

No caravans came down the road to Nottingham. The outlaws had to be patient and wait for spring. To get food, they had to go hunting.

One day, Robin Hood was going through the forest looking for game when he heard a rustling sound in the bushes. "It's a deer," he thought, fitting an arrow into his bow. Then he hid behind a tree—an arrow suddenly came flying and planted itself into the tree, while another passed by whistling, and would certainly have hit Robin in the heart, had he not moved. Surprised, but calm, Robin Hood asked who this could be—maybe one of his merry men, who had left to go hunting and had shot upon hearing a noise?

So, Robin Hood took his own cap, put it on the top of his bow, and held it up high so that it could be seen. Thump! Another arrow planted itself in the tree and went a quarter of the way in. Robin turned. The archer, this time, was right behind him.

He heard a voice, "Robin Hood, you have no escape. Throw down your bow and come out, if you don't want to die like a deer!"

In response, as quick as lightning, Robin pulled back on his bow and let an arrow fly toward the voice. There was a shout in answer.

Robin, crawling in the snow, reached an enormous beech tree. There he stood up and shouted, "Whoever you are, go away or you will not leave this forest alive!"

To answer him, three arrows landed in the tree.

"There are three of them," Robin said to himself, "before there were four." And slowly, he turned to look out carefully. He did not see anyone. But there, just then, a little bird flew off of the branch it had been perched on. Without hesitation, Robin shot an arrow.

There was another shout: another one of the men had been hit.

Several long minutes passed. Robin Hood stood still behind the tree, deciding what to do.

Just then, another arrow hissed by. Robin hit the ground.

Then a voice said, "This time I hit him! Hurrah!"

"The one hundred coins are ours! Come on, tie him to the horse and we'll take him to Nottingham!" Two men appeared from the bushes and moved cautiously toward the beech tree.

Robin Hood jumped to his feet and shot another arrow. One of the two gamekeepers fell to the ground; the other fell to his knees, saying, "Robin, don't kill me, have pity on me!"

"I will not kill you. Pick up your unfortunate companions, tie them to the horses, and go back to the sheriff with my best wishes!"

LITTLE JOHN'S FOLLY

Spring finally arrived.

A great party was held under the Great Oak and it was decided that an archery contest should be held. A hunting knife would be given to the winner.

"But you, Robin," said Friar Tuck, "will be a judge and you cannot shoot. Otherwise, you would win too easily."

Everyone agreed.

The competition began and it was clear that Little John would win.

His arrows all hit the target, however, between one shot and the next he celebrated with a jug of wine. When the contest was over, amid laughter, he went to receive his prize. When he had it in his hands, he shouted, "Ssh! Silence!" "What do you want to say?" someone asked. Raising his arms, he said, "That . . . that I am the greatest archer of Sherwood!"

Scarlet said, "Maybe there is someone who is even better than you, Little John!"

"And who might that be? Robin Hood? No, no!" The giant came forward, took up a bow and forced it into Robin Hood's hands, saying, "Compete with me, if you are a man!"

Alan whispered, "Little John, you'd better stop, and—"

Then something happened that left everyone surprised. The big man turned and landed a punch that sent Alan flat on his back. Putting an arrow into his bow, he said, "Robin, shoot with me or you are a coward!"

With a sigh, Robin cocked an arrow; "What do we shoot at?"

Little John answered, "At our hearts!"

and so saying, he walked backward, putting his shoulders against a tree. "Put yourself against the Great Oak, Robin! And we will begin the contest!" Robin leaned against the tree and shouted, "Go ahead! Shoot!"

"Of course I'll shoot!" responded the big man, and he let an arrow fly . . . that landed in the dirt far from Robin's feet. Robin, then, picking up his bow, said, "Let's see if I can hit the target!"

Marian cried, "Don't kill him!"

Eyeing his target, Robin responded, "Isn't this what he wanted? You want to see how I shoot, Little John? Here!" Everyone shouted as the arrow left Robin's bow.

It imbedded itself in the tree trunk, nailing down a poisonous snake that was about to give a lethal bite to Little John. A shout went up and Robin was carried in triumph, while Little John cried desperately. On his knees he begged, "Forgive me, Robin! I'll never celebrate too much again!"

WHAT HAS HAPPENED TO KING RICHARD?

Meanwhile, from London came news that made the Sheriff of Nottingham and his followers very happy, and filled Robin and the outlaws of Sherwood with sadness.

Since many years had passed, and King Richard the Lion-Hearted had not returned, Prince John was preparing to declare himself king.

"If John becomes king," Marian sighed, "we will never be able to return home!"

"That's true, Marian," Robin answered her, "and the battle between Saxons and Normans will become even worse."

"By now the crusade must have finished quite awhile ago," Friar Tuck murmured, "and the king has not come back. I wonder why?"

What had happened to Richard the Lion-Hearted, and why did he not return? He, Philip Augustus and Frederick the Red-Beard of Germany had gone with the crusaders to the Holy Land, where they battled the Muslims, distinguishing themselves fighting in the battles of Arsuf and Beitnuba. Leading the English, he had conquered the city of Saint John of Acri, penetrating farther. Finally, he had arrived in view of the sacred city of Jerusalem.

Here, his soldiers had seen him raise his shield and cover his face. Surprised, they had asked him what this gesture meant, and he had answered, "Ah, men, I hide my face, so as not to see Jerusalem, which I will not be able to conquer!"

"Why, Sire?"

"Because," he said with melancholy, "our allies have decided to abandon the crusade. The Germans are discouraged by the death of their Emperor, Frederick the Red-Beard, who, alas, drowned in a river. The French obey their king, Philip Augustus, who is, by now, tired of battle."

"But we," the English soldiers, who were both Saxons and Normans, had proudly said, "will stay with you!"

"Yes, my faithful, I know, but alone we will never be able to scale the walls of Jerusalem and pray in Christ's sacred sepulchre."

King Richard had started making treaties with the Muslims, and this resulted in a three-year truce with their king, Saladin the Great. He then began the long journey home with his army, but worried by the news that reached him from England, he left his men, and he hurried toward his homeland followed by only a few men. He had been told that his brother, Prince John, planned to strip him of the throne by proclaiming himself king, and that under his rule the Norman tyranny over the Saxons had been encouraged. From that time on, news of Richard was vague and uncertain. Someone said that he had reached Friuli, where he had left for Germany; others said that he had headed for France, and still others said that he had sailed from Venice.

Essentially, there was no trace of King Richard. What had happened to him? Was he already dead? Was he still alive? And if he was still alive, why did he not return?

THE KNIGHT WITH NO MONEY

One day, a knight was seen crossing the forest. The men of Sherwood were lying in ambush, and a minute later, the knight, wearing fine shiny armor, approached. He was followed by a mule led by a servant.

Robin came out of the bushes saying, "Stop, sir!"

The knight obeyed, and asked, "Why do you want me to stop?"

"Because you are passing through an area of the forest filled with outlaws and danger."

"I am not afraid of outlaws or danger!"

"I am quite sure of that. But before confronting them, wouldn't you like to dine with us?"

"Ah," said the knight with a smile, "that I would like very much."

"Follow me, then," replied Robin, and he guided the knight to the Great Oak, under which the long table was ready. Everyone made the new arrival feel welcome, and they ate. When the last goblet of wine was empty, Robin said, "Sir, I hope that this meal was pleasant for you." "Oh, very pleasant!" he replied. "Good!" said Robin Hood. "You see, we are honored to have a guest like you, but we are too poor to offer such a meal for free. Therefore, you must pay us."

The knight nodded and said, "Fair enough. But, the trouble is that I have no money."

"Impossible!" exclaimed Little John.

"Unfortunately, it is so. I have only what I am wearing, the horse, the mule, and my old servant. I have nothing else." The knight opened the purse on his belt. It was empty.

Robin said, "Strange, to see such a poor knight."

"It is at that," said the other sadly. "During a tournament, my lance broke, and a piece broke away so hard that it hit one of my companions in the heart. In short, I killed a man and I had to compensate his widow, for which I got money from a money lender, and to pay him back I had to sell everything I had. I should go to pay the last installment, but as you see I have no money, and so I will be sent to prison."

A long silence followed. Then a voice shouted, "Who said that a money lender can put a good knight in prison?" Robin continued, "How much do you owe that usurer?"

"Three hundred gold coins."

"You shall have them! Scarlet, bring a purse with three hundred coins! We take money from the rich to give to the poor. Even if you are a knight, you are poor. So, go pay the usurer, and be at peace!" That was how the outlaws of Sherwood behaved.

BETRAYAL!

When it was spring, the Sheriff of Nottingham came into the forest with a long line of soldiers. They were led by a traitor; he was the coward who had sent the four gamekeepers to kill Robin in the snow-covered forest.

Sure of himself, the traitor had gone to the Sheriff of Nottingham and reached an agreement with him.

He knew Sherwood Forest well, and presented himself to the sentries, who stood on guard at night here and there in the forest, befriending them and offering them all something to drink. Trusting him, they drank and a little while later, they fell into a deep sleep. In the heart of night, then, the traitor led the sheriff toward the Great Oak. Here, Robin slept beside Marian.

In a second his sleep was interrupted, and he sat bolt upright in alarm, without knowing why. He thought, "It is as if I felt that there were some danger nearby . . ."

He waited a little while, then, getting up, said, "Yes, I sense danger. Friends,

alert!" he shouted.

The camp was immediately awake, and everyone got up, wondering what was happening.

Friar Tuck came running. "What is it, Robin? What—?"

He could not finish.

A shout was heard, "Prince John and the Sheriff of Nottingham!"

The soldiers came out from everywhere. There was no possibility of resistance. To avoid a slaughter, Robin Hood put up his hands and exclaimed, "I surrender, friends! Do as I do!"

The sheriff arrived just then. Sneering, he said, "See, bandit? Finally, I have beaten you!"

Then he ordered his men. "Go ahead, men! Tie them up, and tie them up good! At dawn, they will all be hanged from their Great Oak Tree!"

THE OUTLAWS' COMEBACK

A little while later, the outlaws were sitting on the ground, with their hands tied behind their backs. The sheriff's men surrounded them, with lances in hand, on guard.

A sinister rosy light lit the scene as the merry men's cabins and refuges burned.

Passing before them on horseback, the sheriff had exclaimed, "I am going to Nottingham and I will be back with enough rope to hang all of you!"

Friar Tuck whispered, "Come on, let's all join in prayer like good Christians." The outlaws then began to pray, while the stars quickly disappeared and a vague brightness in the east announced dawn.

At a certain point, one of the sheriff's men, who was wearing armor, came to the group of prisoners with heavy steps, and said in a loud voice, "Where is Robin Hood? I want to see him and hang him, that bandit! Ah, here you are!" he said then, stopping in front of Robin, "Take, this!" He landed a punch, then another, then another. "Take this, too!" he punched him again, and, sneering, he went amid shouts of anger and curses from the outlaws. Robin had been thrown to the ground in the fury. Bending over him, Marian cried desperately, "Oh, Robin—"

"Shhh, my wife. He gave me three good punches, yes ... but he also gave me this!" and he showed her the knife that, between one punch and another, the knight had hidden under his cloak and secretly passed to Robin.

Word was passed, and all the outlaws got ready. There was no time to lose. Robin, in a low voice, ordered Little

44

John to put himself back-to-back with him, and with the knife he cut the cords that bound his friend's hands. Little John first freed Robin, then quickly Marian and Edith, and then the bravest outlaws. Everyone stayed seated, though, so as not to let on to anything.

Robin whispered, "At my command, everyone against the sentries, with their weapons, then, we get the others. Listen up," he said, tensing his muscles, "Now!" And he shouted this last word as he launched himself at a guard; before they knew what was happening, the sheriff's men found themselves under attack.

They tried to resist, then they threw down their arms, and vanished into the forest.

When the sheriff returned with great coils of rope, there was no longer even a shadow of the merry men beneath the Great Oak.

HOW THE KNIGHT
PAID HIS DEBT

Later on, Robin Hood and his companions returned under the Great Oak. Robin Hood spoke to them. "Before anything else, friends, we must understand how they were able to surprise and capture us like that."

Everyone went into the forest, and at the guard posts they found the sentries still sleeping.

"They have been drugged," said Robin.

"Who do you think it could have been?" asked Little John.

Robin answered, "We will know when our friends wake up. But there is something else I would like to know. Who was it that gave me that knife, and saved our lives?"

When the sentries awoke, they said it had been a hunter who had offered them drink. Just then they heard the sound of hooves and the merry men hid themselves on the path, stopping a knight on horseback. It was the poor knight, to whom Robin had given the money.

He said smiling, "Hello, friends! I must tell you three things. The first is that, thanks to your money, I am not only free, but I got back my modest castle and my lands."

Robin asked, "And the second?"

"That's a little sad. A hunter was

46

hanged this morning in Nottingham on the orders of the sheriff. Why, I don't know, but I heard the sheriff accuse him of having helped you, Robin Hood, escape, and of having betrayed him as he had betrayed you. What could the sheriff have meant?"

Little John exclaimed, "The hunter paid for his betrayal."

Robin Hood asked the knight, "And what is the third thing?"

"That I was very sorry to have punched you, Robin. But how else could I have given you the knife?"

"Aha!" exclaimed Robin Hood, "It was you, then, who saved us?"

"When I found out that the sheriff was preparing to trick you, I mixed myself in with his men." Robin Hood shook the knight's hand and asked, "Why did you do that, my friend?"

The other replied, "To pay my debt."

Then he got back on his horse and left.

47

TWO GREEDY FRIARS

Once Alan said to Friar Tuck, "Why do you live with the outlaws?"

"I am here only because you do not rob for yourselves, but for the poor. Whether I am making a mistake or not," and Friar Tuck raised his eyes toward the sky, "I will leave for God to judge. But don't think that all friars are like me. Many are greedy, and they are concerned only with snatching as much money as they can."

That same day, Robin Hood was sitting in a tree when he saw two friars coming down the path on their mules. He said to himself, "Those are the greedy friars of whom Tuck spoke," and with a leap, he was on the path. "Peace be with you," he said. A friar replied, "Who are you?" Robin Hood said, "I am a poor man, and you have two full sacks on your mules. Wouldn't you have a coin or two for me?" "In these sacks there is only dry bread for the poor," said the second friar, "and not a single coin, so, step aside."

Robin exclaimed, "Well then, there are three of us without any money!"

"Pray, and the good Lord will send you some money. Now, move, we are in a hurry," said the friars. "Right!" said Robin without moving. "I will pray, and, since the three of us are poor, let us pray together. Get on your knees! I'm sure that the good Lord will send us something!" He smiled, but he spoke with a vaguely threatening tone. The two friars were afraid and thought it was better not to contradict him, so they obeyed him, got down on their knees beside Robin, and pretended to pray. They were there when Little John came down the path and, seeing the three on their knees with their hands together, asked with surprise, "What are you all doing?"

"We are praying," answered Robin. Little John pointed to the friars' sacks and said, "Is it possible that there is not even a single coin in here?"

"There is only dry bread for the poor," Robin told him. "Come and pray with us." Understanding that this was a joke, the big man got down on his knees. A good hour passed like this, and finally, Robin said to the friars, "What do you say? Has the good Lord sent us some money?"

"Look in your pockets and you will know," replied a friar. Robin put his hands in his pockets and exclaimed, "Nothing! And you, Little John?"

"Nothing! But maybe, the good Lord put something in the pockets of these friars." "Friars don't have pockets, you fool!" exclaimed a friar. Robin Hood said, "Well, then, he would have put something in your sacks. Little John, go see if a coin or two comes out of those sacks!" "Leave the sacks alone!" shouted the friars, but Little John had already opened them. They were full of coins.

Closing them, he said, "Nothing, only dry bread." "See?" said the friars, "Can we go now?" "Of course you can go," said Robin, "but, since there is dry bread for the poor in your bags, and we are poor, we will take the sacks." The two friars paled. "It is very charitable of you," said Robin, "to give us this dry bread. Little John, take the sacks. Good-bye, friars, and have a good trip." And with that, the two outlaws disappeared into the forest.

THE THREE NORMAN BROTHERS

One day a woman came to the Great Oak. She dropped to her knees before Robin and sighing, said, "Robin Hood, help me! Even if I am a Norman, help me!" A great silence fell, and Robin asked, "Norman or Saxon, woman, makes no difference. Tell me what has happened to you."

Tears running down her face, she said she was a widow with three young sons, all good young men but, alas, hotheads; they drank to the health of King Richard in a tavern, were arrested, and brought to Nottingham. "The sheriff has condemned them to death, Robin Hood, and tomorrow they will be hanged in the square!" concluded the woman desperately. Robin Hood answered, "You can be sure that no one will be hanged." Then he called together all his faithful men to decide what to do.

That same evening, three friars presented themselves at the gates of Nottingham, asking to be allowed to enter the city. "I am Friar Tuck," said one of them. "I must guide my brothers to the convent of Saint Dunstan."

The sentry let them pass, without suspecting that, together with Friar Tuck, he had allowed Scarlet and Alan to pass as well. At another gate, a little later, a Norman knight presented himself, and with a proud gesture, ordered, "Open up. I am Sir Gideon of Gideon, and I have come with my squire to watch the hanging."

"Go ahead," said the guards, and thus, Midge, another friend of Robin Hood's, entered Nottingham, followed by Little John. At a third gate, a one-eyed cripple dressed with rags approached. In a hoarse voice, he asked, "I heard that tomorrow three rebels will be hanged. Is it true?"

"Yes, it is true, but what does it matter to you?" answered the guard.

"I am interested only because I am an executioner. There is no one better than me, so I come to offer my services to the sheriff. Take me to him." The guards spoke between themselves. One finally said, "All right, come with me," and he took the cripple to the sheriff who, with a cruel smile, said,

"Ah, you say you have hanged many people, eh?" "Yes, one hundred and two people, all enemies of Prince John. I am," said the cripple, "Billy the executioner. You must have heard of me!" "All right, you will hang them. Now go away," said the sheriff. Holding out a dirty hand, Billy replied, "Yes, but you must pay me first. Three hangings, three coins."

"Maddock," said the sheriff, "pay this miserable fellow." Maddock did so, not knowing he was paying Robin Hood.

THE BATTLE AT THE GALLOWS

The next morning, a cart pulled by two oxen came out from the castle and slowly moved toward the square.

It was escorted by the sheriff's guards, and it carried three young men with pale and proud faces, with their hands tied behind their backs.

The good residents of Nottingham had preferred to stay at home, so as not to have to witness another execution. However, there was no lack of people around the gallows. The sheriff's blacksmiths had worked all night to prepare them. Three nooses hung from a large beam supported by two heavy poles. The young men would have to put their heads into these, and at a signal from the sheriff, the executioner, assisted by a blow from a hammer, would make the wooden trapdoor, on which the men stood, fall in.

Many women, who had been forced to stay in the square, were crying.

Groups of men were silent and dark-faced. But here and there, the sheriff's faithful raised their fists, shouting, "Come on, hurry up! Get ready, Billy!"

"Leave everything to me!" said the executioner and, limping onto the platform, he faced the nooses and the boards. Taking quick glances around from time to time, he saw that the men upon whom he was counting were in their places. He shouted to the crowd, "Now you will see what I am capable of doing!" A drumroll was heard, and the cart with the condemned came slowly forward to stop right in front of the platform. The three young men were made to get out and were pushed toward the gallows. There was a great silence. Shortly, the sheriff and Sir Maddock arrived, followed by their Norman courtiers. Raising his hand with the iron glove, the sheriff said, "Begin, Billy!"

"I am ready!" responded the executioner, and one by one he organized the nooses around the young men's necks. He did it with rude and violent gestures, meanwhile whispering, "Pretend you don't hear anything. Don't worry, you are not going to die; I have arranged the knots so that the nooses will slip when the trapdoor you are standing on opens. Under the platform, you will find three swords. Take them up and battle with me for your lives." Turning then to the sheriff, he shouted, "Sir, I am ready!"

"Fine! Everyone, see how I punish enemies of our prince! Sound the drums! And when I raise my right hand, you, executioner, will make your stroke!"

The gong sounded loudly; everyone looked at the sheriff.

He raised his hand. With a huge mallet, the executioner hit the trapdoor, which fell in. The young men dangled in the air, but only for a moment. The nooses, instead of tightening around their necks, slipped, and the young men fell.

They got right back up and threw themselves under the platform. "Betrayal!" shouted the sheriff. The executioner threw off his cloak and showed that he was not an old cripple, but a strong young man with a sword in his hands. "Who is this traitor?" asked the sheriff. A loud voice shouted, "It's Robin Hood!"

A STRANGE ESCAPE

"Robin Hood!" exclaimed the stupefied sheriff. "Get him! Get him!" But in that instant, the three young men jumped onto the platform and they too went to battle. They put themselves beside Robin Hood, and with great slashes drove back the sheriff's men who were trying to climb the platform steps.

Watching, Sir Maddock shouted, "Surround them, they cannot escape, there are only four of them!" But in response, several arrows came singing past him, hitting some of his soldiers.

Everyone turned to see who had shot, and there, on a roof, were Friar Tuck, Scarlet, Midge, and Little John; the merry companions, who, disguised, had entered Nottingham. "Robin Hood! Robin Hood!" they shouted, shooting more arrows. The crowd got excited and frightened shouts went up. A general scuffle ensued and in the confusion the horses went out of control, and the frightened oxen overturned the cart as they tried to move. Under the rain of arrows, the sheriff's men could do nothing but back off. Even the sheriff and Sir Maddock retired. Sir Maddock, however, overcame his

surprise enough to recover his courage and ordered, "Go ahead, soldiers! Half on one side, against the platform, the other half against the archers! Get them!"

The soldiers moved forward, but no one could be seen on the platform. Taking advantage of the confusion, Robin Hood and the three young men had disappeared.

Sir Maddock shouted, "Where did they go?" He certainly could not have imagined that they had gone up the stairs of a house whose door had been left open and onto the roof to join the group of archers. When they were among their own, Robin said, "Great, friends, but now let's get out of here! Quickly!"

"Follow me!" responded Midge, "I know the way!"

Jumping from rooftop to rooftop, the outlaws set off for one of the gates of Nottingham, while the sheriff's men searched for them in the streets.

"Where are they, Maddock?" cried the sheriff. "They disappeared right under our noses!"

"Yes," said Sir Maddock, "but they have to pass through the gates of the city, and we will close them all!" Several horsemen galloped off to give orders, and all the gates were locked and guarded by soldiers. The streets were evacuated. Nottingham seemed a city of the dead. "Robin Hood came to Nottingham, yes, but he won't be able to leave! The mouse went and put himself in a trap!" exclaimed the sheriff.

He certainly could not have imagined that Robin and his men had already left the city of Nottingham and were running toward the forest. How had they escaped?

They had jumped down from the rooftops, and then Midge led them down a dried-out well. From there, they wended their way along dark, narrow passages that were actually the ancient Roman sewer system. Everyone had forgotten about them; everyone except Midge.

After some time, the men came up through another dried well into a field outside the city, and headed straight for the forest. So, while the sheriff and his men waited in vain by the gates, the merry men began to celebrate under the Great Oak.

WELCOME TO SHERWOOD

It was early autumn when Midge returned from London, where he had gone to visit his old aunt, and he told his companions seated under the Great Oak all he had learned in the great capital. There was a good deal of uncertainty and unrest. No more news had been heard of King Richard, and the rumor was that he was dead by now. Thus, Prince John had decided to crown himself king. But most of England's nobles did not agree with John. "Old King Henry's sons," they said, "are Richard and John. The crown goes to the first-born, therefore, Richard was proclaimed king. John is not the legitimate royal heir, and if he takes the throne, he will be an usurper."

The partisans of John responded, "But King Richard is dead, so, his younger brother is the legitimate heir." "Who says that King Richard is dead?" others argued. "If he were not dead, he would have come back; the crusade has been over for several years," was the reply.

"What would happen if King Richard were to return?" To this, John's partisans shrugged their shoulders and did not answer.

"They do not speak, the cowards," Midge said, "and they do not dare say that if King Richard were to return, the prince's assassins would kill him."

A long silence followed, then Robin Hood said, "God forbid that King Richard should be dead. If he is alive and he should return, we will defend him."

Several weeks went by and nothing happened. The days passed quietly, and the leaves began to lose their splendor; the sun set earlier and rose later each day.

It was nearly dawn when one of the sentries announced that a caravan had taken the main road through the forest. Robin Hood immediately assembled his men. "If a caravan is on the main road," he said, "it is made up of rich merchants or warriors: either we will have a good haul, or a good fight. Let's be ready, and let's welcome these people who have entered our forest."

In a short time, with their quivers filled with arrows, the outlaws had prepared for an ambush. Robin ordered that no one disturb the caravan as it came into the forest. Everything would be quiet and calm, and the travelers would not imagine that there was any danger.

But where the road narrowed, a trap was planned, and the men in green would jump from the trees. Taken from the front, back, and sides at once, the members of the caravan, whether merchants or soldiers, would have to stop.

Imitating the dry knocks of a woodpecker, Scarlet signaled that the last horse had passed. Shortly, the guide leading the caravan appeared, and behind him three knights, some loaded mules, and other people on horseback.

Seated on the branch of a old beech tree, Robin waited for all of them to pass by. Then he blew his horn loudly, jumped down, and said, "Gentlemen, welcome to Sherwood!"

THE RETURN OF RICHARD THE LION-HEARTED

Stepping forward, Robin said, "We do not want to hurt you, do not fear!" The knight, with the visor of his helmet lowered, responded with a firm, deep voice, "We are not afraid of you. But if you do not want to hurt us, why do you have your bows ready to shoot?"

"One can never be too prudent, sir," replied the outlaw with a smile. He asked, "Could you by any chance all be friends of the Sheriff of Nottingham?"

The knight began to laugh. "No, no!" he said. "We don't even know who the Sheriff of Nottingham is! But you, why is it that you have interrupted our journey?"

"Because we would like to invite you, sir, and your companions, to dine with us under the great oak tree."

The knight, at whose side the other two knights had come to stand, answered, "By Jove, if that's it, friend, we accept heartily! I am very hungry, and I believe my companions feel the same! Let's go!"

So the caravan interrupted its journey and leaving the road, took a path into the forest and arrived at the Great Oak. The long table had been arranged. All around, several spits were being turned to prepare delicious roast wild game.

The knight stopped his horse before a giant spit and said, "But this is royal deer, property of the king. How were you allowed to hunt it?"

"You see, sir, since good King Richard the Lion-Hearted left, there is really no longer a king in England; therefore, the deer belong to everyone and that is why we hunt them."

"I see. And what if King Richard were to return?"

"Then we would not hunt them anymore, because we would no longer live in the forest. King Richard would rule with justice, unlike Prince John and the Sheriff of Nottingham. But enough talk. We came here to eat. Sit down, gentlemen, and take off your helmets."

The knight sat down, but he did not take off his helmet. He said, "You just spoke of the Sheriff of Nottingham. Is he an enemy of King Richard?" "A sworn enemy of the king and ours, too!"

"And you?" asked the knight.

"We are faithful to the king and are certain that one day he will return."

"And if he returned, what would you do?" queried the knight.

"On my honor," said Alan, "we would fight under his orders!"

"Yes!" shouted the merry men.

The knight took off his helmet and said, "Then I hope you are ready! I am Richard, King of England!"

RICHARD IN NOTTINGHAM

At these words, all the men of the forest fell to their knees bowing their heads, and Robin said in a loud voice, "God save the king!"

Richard the Lion-Hearted ordered, "Get up, my friends. Stand up, Robin Hood."

Obeying, the archer asked, "Then, Sire, you must know who I am?"

With a smile, the king answered, "I heard talk of the merry men of Sherwood and their leader even down in the Holy Land. I returned to England in disguise, and I came to Sherwood because I know that here I have friends. In a few weeks, I will gather all my followers in the city of Sheffield and from there I will march on London. Friends," he continued, "would you come with me to Nottingham?"

"To Nottingham! To Nottingham!" echoed the merry men.

Richard turned to Robin. "We will take the city by storm. There are not many of us, but fortune always favors the brave."

"Excuse me, Sire," responded Robin

Hood, "but I think that there are truly too few of us to attack the city."

"And how, then, do you intend to enter the city?" asked Richard. Robin explained that he thought they could enter Nottingham by taking the route that Midge had taught them, that is, through the sewers. Richard knit his brows. But the next day the two sentries who stood on guard at the castle saw a man, and then another, come up out of the ground. Not believing their eyes, they hurried to the sheriff and shouted, "Sir, alert! We are under attack!" The sheriff, who was seated at dinner with Sir Maddock, started and asked, "And who is attacking us? Where do they come from, these enemies?"

"From underground, sir!"

"Oh? Four good whippings and you won't see ghosts anymore!"

Just then, a voice said, "Do I too seem like a ghost?"

"King Richard!" exclaimed the two at the same time, standing up.

King Richard had, in fact, appeared on the threshold of the room.

THE END
OF THE SHERIFF

When he recovered his voice, the sheriff knelt before the king and implored, "Spare my life! I have always been faithful to you; I have always served you with devotion, Sire, and if I obeyed your brother Prince John it is only because he reigned over the kingdom of England in your name!" King Richard then said, "I know you have lied. But even if you had been faithful, you have abused your position. You have humiliated the good citizens of Nottingham and sent many to the gallows."

"But, they were all your enemies, Sire!"

"Oh yes? And what about those that you stole from?"

"They were enemies, too!"

"Hmm, but you found their money to be friendly! You are greedy!"

Pale, the sheriff found the courage to protest, "Ah, Sire, but who told you all these lies? Who spoke to you of me?"

"It was Robin Hood who told me of all your bad deeds," answered Richard. The sheriff ground his teeth and exclaimed, "Robin Hood! That bandit, that cowardly Saxon! He lies, Sire! He is afraid of me and tries to ruin me with words, not daring to confront me with the sword!" "Is he afraid of you, or are you afraid of him?" asked Richard.

"Me, afraid?" exclaimed the sheriff. "If Robin Hood were here—" He was suddenly silent, because on the threshold, to the right of the king, Robin Hood had appeared. Richard said, "What would you do if Robin Hood were here? Would you challenge him to a duel for being a liar? Well, fine, go ahead and do just that, now!" Trembling like a leaf, the sheriff stuttered, "I - I … Sire, a representative of the king cannot do battle with a bandit!" Entering the room and sitting down, Richard said, "I give you permission. You will do battle here and right away. Go ahead," he added, nodding toward two large swords hanging on a wall,

"those are the weapons."
Since he had no way out, the sheriff gathered his courage and decided to battle to the death. As for Robin Hood, the sword wasn't his preferred weapon, but he was not afraid, sure as he was of his strength.

At a signal from the king, the duel began. The sheriff attacked first, slashing out with his sword. Robin Hood drew back as the blade grazed him. When the sheriff made a false move, Robin took the offensive, moving in on his rival.

The sound of blades clashing woke all of Nottingham. In front of the sheriff's castle, a curious crowd had formed.

When it was discovered that the duel was between the sheriff and Robin Hood, the crowd became very excited. Meanwhile, the duellists continued their battle, following one another from room to room.

Robin stumbled and fell many times, as did his adversary, and at one point it seemed that the battle would end because both were too tired to go on.

Finally, Robin Hood's sword flashed like lightning and pierced right through the sheriff's heart. He gave a shout, let his weapon fall, and crumbled to the floor. That was the end of the Sheriff of Nottingham.

ROBERT, COUNT OF HUNTINGDON

Within a few months, Richard had regained his rightful place on the throne of England. Now, Robin and the outlaws of Sherwood could return home. Everyone gathered under the Great Oak to say good-bye. "I'm going back to Fountain Abbey to sing praises to God and to celebrate mass," said Friar Tuck.

Alan Dale said, "I will go with my wife, Edith, from castle to castle to sing songs. And you, Robin, what will you do? Where will you go?" With the beautiful Marian at his side, Robin said, "I don't know, I have never had a home. When I was very young I lived at Marian's house, but I cannot return there. Her brother lives there now, and besides, it's too small ... What will I do? I really don't know."

Marian said, "The good Lord will send us a sign, friends."

In that very moment, a knight came riding into the clearing carrying the royal flag and said, "King Richard has sent me!"

"Welcome. What does the king want from us?" asked Robin Hood.

The messenger answered, "He wants the Count of Huntingdon to go to London with him right away."

"There's no count here," said Midge.

Robin, in fact, had never revealed to anyone, not even to Marian, that he was the son of the Count of Huntingdon. The messenger said, "These are the king's orders!" and he turned the horse around and disappeared into the forest. The merry men were completely perplexed.

Friar Tuck said, "If the king orders, one must respond. Go to London, Robin, and explain to Richard that there is no Count of Huntingdon among us." Embarrassed, Robin obeyed. While all the outlaws left the forest to return to their homes, he, with Marian and Little John, set off for London. After traveling for a month, they arrived at the royal castle. King Richard greeted Robin in the best of ways, he shook his hand, invited him to dine with him, seated him on his right, showed him his horses, truly celebrating his presence. Robin finally said to him, "Sire, you asked for the Count of Huntingdon, but he is not among us, in Sherwood."

"What? You're kidding me, Robin!"

"Sire, Robin Hood would never kid you!" said the beautiful Marian.

King Richard sighed, "So, Robin," he exclaimed, "you never even told your own wife!" "Marian," he continued, "Robin wanted to be like all his companions, but in reality, he is of noble blood."

"Oh, Robin!" exclaimed Marian.

Richard ordered, "Robin, down on your knees before me!"

Unsettled and perplexed, Robin obeyed. King Richard unsheathed his sword and laid it gently on one of Robin's shoulders. Then he solemnly said, "My faithful Robin Hood, from this moment on you are once again in possession of the castle and the lands that your forefathers possessed, and as of this moment, you are Robert, Count of Huntingdon."

THE DEATH OF KING RICHARD

Thus, Robin returned as master of his family's property. The castle of Huntingdon had been reduced to a pile of bricks, but he rebuilt it, aided by his old companions and also by the residents of Nottingham, who remembered him for his battle with the sheriff. In less than a year the castle was ready and Robin went to live there.

They were days of great festivity, and the times that followed were also serene, until the day a messenger covered with dust arrived at the castle. He announced, "Count, King Richard calls all his faithful to arms, because war has broken out against the King of France." "I am ready!" answered Robin. "I will gather my men and meet the king in London."

"You will meet him in France," said the messenger, "because the king has already left and is already fighting even now. Good-bye!"

Robin Hood had his friends called. Little John arrived first, then Scarlet, Midge, and Alan Dale; from Fountain Abbey came Friar Tuck, and slowly all those who had been the merry men of the forest arrived at Huntingdon.

They still had not left to join the king, however, when more unfortunate news reached them: King Richard the Lion-Hearted had died in battle. Once he arrived in France, the impetuous king had pushed to the interior, but he had found a castle that blocked his way. He had attacked, sure of conquering it quickly, but the defenders had resisted courageously and Richard could do nothing but lay siege. But even the siege was prolonged. The king, impatient, and furious with his enemies' resistance, had begun to battle frequently as a simple soldier, sometimes pushing until he was under the wall and exposing himself to his adversaries' offensives. His advisers had reprimanded him for this, saying, "You are not just any foot soldier, you are the king. You must be careful." Richard said, "I have always fought in the front, and I have always been fortunate. I shall be so here, too!"

Alas, this time things went much differently. Having gone too close to the castle, the king was hit in the shoulder by an enemy arrow. He was rescued, and at the time the wound had not seemed serious, but later it developed an infection that the doctors could not cure.

Within a few days, Richard had expired. An appalled silence fell over the camp, and very soon, quiet fell over all of England, which found itself without its beloved king. What would happen, now?

Many feared that the nobles would fight one another for the throne, but this did not happen, because everyone, willingly or not, recognized that Prince John, after his brother's death, was the legitimate heir to England's crown.

John took the throne, promising to reign with justice and moderation. It was not this way. Before long, his arrogant Norman friends returned to power, and a wind of discord blew over England.

FIRE IN THE CASTLE

A few weeks after John's return, about twenty knights presented themselves in front of Robin's castle. One of them shouted, "Count of Huntingdon, the castle and the lands are no longer yours. You must leave, by order of the king and the new Sheriff of Nottingham. You," continued the knight, mocking, "surely remember him. He is Sir Maddock who sends word that you must be out by tonight, or he will come with five hundred men, and hang you and all of yours!" and so saying, the knight left.

With great sadness, Marian and Robin took what they could carry and loaded it onto a cart. They were loading the last of their things when the cruel Sir Maddock appeared before the castle, followed by a dozen of his men.

Sneering, he said, "Hurry up, or I'll have you driven away and beaten! I am going to live in this castle!"

Pale with rage, Robin ordered his men, "Continue to prepare the cart. I must do some other work," and he left. Around sunset the drawbridge was lowered and the cart, driven by Robin Hood, left the castle amid laughter and words of scorn from the sheriff's men. Marian, trying to hold back her tears, murmured, "Oh, Robin, how bitter it is to be defeated like this! How sad it is to think that this castle will be Maddock's!"

Robin answered, "This castle will not belong to anyone."

Marian did not understand what her husband meant. She found out, though, within a few hours. In fact, when it was night, Robin returned to the castle in which Sir Maddock was already having a great party; cautiously he crept nearer, with his faithful bow in hand. Once there he cocked an arrow dipped in pitch.

He lit it, and launched the flaming arrow, which went in through a window and planted itself in a pile of dry wood, also covered in flammable pitch, which Robin had prepared that afternoon.

In a few minutes, the fire spread and the whole castle was engulfed in flames. To the rosy light that reverberated all over, Robin shouted, "Now you may have my castle, Maddock!"

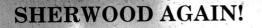

SHERWOOD AGAIN!

Sherwood Forest was quiet.
Marian whispered, "Robin, this silence is almost frightening."
"Don't be afraid, Marian. The forest has always protected us."
"But, everything will be different. We will no longer have our merry companions," said Marian.
"Everything will be different, yes," responded Robin Hood, "but nothing has changed, only the grass has covered the paths. It is like going back in time. We will miss our friends. But at least we can live safely here, and Maddock will not be able to hurt us." After a few hours they reached the Great Oak.

The grass had grown very tall in the clearing, and the wild vines had covered the huts with their green embrace.

Robin said with a smile, "Here's a job for you, Marian. You can clear the weeds from the hut, while I find something to eat."

Robin then left to go hunting. When he saw a wild boar by a brook, he loaded his bow in silence, eyed the boar, and shot his arrow. Without even a moan, the poor beast fell to the ground. Coming out of the bush where he had been hidden, Robin went over to it. To his surprise, the animal had two arrows planted in it! "Someone else is here!" he thought, when he heard a voice say, "Hey! That wild boar is mine! Get away from there!"

Not seeing anyone, Robin answered, "And who says so? I hit it with my arrow, therefore, it is mine!"

"Oh, yes? Let's see, then!"

"Of course we'll see! Come out, whoever you are, and if you want we'll fight for the boar!"

"Here I am!" shouted the voice, and from the trees jumped a man. He stopped and exclaimed, "Robin!"

"Little John!"

The two embraced, and asked one another, "Why are you here?" and laughed because they had spoken at the same time.

Robin told his story and Little John said, "Yes, I, too, left my home because of Maddock's bullying. He must be persecuting all those who were on poor King Richard's side."

"Anyway, if he comes to Sherwood, we'll give him his. Come on, let's go! We'll take turns carrying the boar." And so they returned together to the Great Oak.

FIFTEEN COINS

Before arriving at their old meeting place the two stopped, perplexed, and Little John asked in a low voice, "What is that noise?"

Robin laughed happily and answered, "That is not a noise, Little John, it is a sound. Remember? Years ago you asked me the very same question and I gave you the same answer!"

"But then, it is—"

"Yes, it is the sound of a harp, and that is Alan Dale!" Running, Robin and Little John arrived at the Great Oak, and together with Marian were Edith and Alan! There was a grand party. The festivities grew when,

one by one, the merry men returned. Midge came back, Friar Tuck came back, Scarlet came back, and all the others. They had returned to Sherwood Forest to escape the sheriff's persecution.

Then Robin exclaimed, "Well, friends, now it will be Maddock who will be persecuted!"

"Hurrah! Hurrah!" they all shouted.

One day, the lookouts announced that an abbot was coming down the road carried by his servants in a rich sedan-chair.

Robin said, "Great, I will invite him to dine with us. Prepare something to eat, Marian!"

A while later, Robin Hood jumped onto the road from a tree. The little

caravan stopped, and the abbot, poking his bald head from the sedan-chair, asked, "What is it?"

"I am Robin Hood, blessed abbot, and I invite you to dine with me."

"Eat?" said the abbot, "Let's go! I'm very hungry!"

At the end of the meal, as usual, Robin told the abbot that he had to pay for all that he had eaten. The abbot replied, "You should know that I have only fifteen gold coins, and nothing else. I am a poor abbot."

Alan said, "Abbot, yes, but poor, it does not seem."

"I have only fifteen coins! Go ahead and look in my bags!"

Robin said, "No. If you have only fifteen coins, we will not take them. You may go, poor and saintly abbot."

"All right, good-bye!" said the abbot and climbing into his sedan-chair, he ordered his servants, "Get moving!" He thought, "Robin Hood thinks he is clever, but I am smarter than he!"

Scarlet said, "Robin, that abbot was a liar! I do not believe he had only fifteen coins! Why didn't you look in his bags?"

Robin Hood answered with a smile, "Because there were only fifteen coins in his bags. Hidden under the sedan-chair, however, in a leather pouch, there were two hundred coins. Here they are!" He emptied a shower of gold coins onto the table. "The abbot will not complain. We left him the fifteen coins that he swore he had. He didn't realize that I took his bag, and he will be certain to think he is cleverer than I am."

ABDUL AND AHMED

Before long, the news reached London that Robin Hood and his brigade of brigands had again taken to laying their trap on the Sherwood road. King John ordered Sir Maddock to capture the bandits and punish them without pity. Sir Maddock then promised a reward of three hundred coins for the man who brought in Robin Hood, dead or alive. Three hundred gold coins! That was a very high reward. It was natural, then, that more than one person was ready to risk his neck for it. As in the times of the old sheriff, there were those who tried to penetrate Sherwood Forest to reach the outlaws' camp. Robin Hood was in grave danger when Abdul and Ahmed presented themselves to Sir Maddock, Sheriff of Nottingham. They were both Saracens captured by King Richard's crusaders and brought from the Holy Land as slaves to England, where they were finally freed. They were cruel men, whom slavery had made even meaner and more pitiless. Ahmed said to the sheriff, "Show us where we can find your enemy and we will bring you his head."

Sir Maddock responded, "My enemy can be found in Sherwood Forest, which is easy to enter but from which it is difficult to leave."

Ahmed, drawing his scimitar, responded, "Never fear. We will leave from there."

"Watch yourselves. Robin Hood is an infallible archer." Abdul then took his bow from his back, quickly cocked an arrow, and shot it, hitting a swallow that was flying past the castle. He asked with a treacherous smile, "As infallible as I am?" That same night, dressed in black so as to be invisible in the darkness, the two moved into the forest. Alas, they marked their path with blood. Quiet as a snake, Ahmed surprised one of Robin's lookouts and slashed his throat. Abdul followed one of the outlaws and pierced his heart with an arrow as he bent down to drink from a spring.

The next morning, when the two outlaws were found dead, there was consternation and dismay among Robin Hood and his men.

"A black arrow," murmured Robin, "has never been seen here. Among these trees hides an enemy who is hunting us."

Suddenly, a black arrow came whistling out of the forest and killed one of the men. Everyone dropped to the ground, but when they crept to where the arrow had come from, they found no one. Midge said, "Come on! Let's call everyone, and find these assassins!" "No," said Robin. "With so many of us, we'll find nothing." "Well, then?" asked Midge. "I will go alone. If they think they can hunt me, they are wrong. I have never been the game, only the hunter. Return to the Great Oak and stay on guard. I am going hunting!" said Robin, and he disappeared into the trees.

A HUNT TO THE DEATH

For the whole day, Robin went throughout the forest in search of his mysterious enemies.

He passed from a clearing to a forest of birch trees, from the brambles to the fields, from oak groves to beech trees. With watchful eyes he looked, ready to take in even the smallest sign that someone had been there: a broken branch, trampled grass, a crumpled bush. But he found nothing. Even the birds in the trees were singing; it was a sign that no one was there.

Robin stopped suddenly. A web that a spider had spun between a bush and a small plant was broken. "It could have been an animal," he told himself. But his instinct as a man of the forest told him that someone had passed through there. He got down on his knees to look at the ground. Where it was damp, a footprint could be seen. His enemies had come through here. Quietly, Robin pulled an arrow from his quiver and put it in his bow.

It was completely silent.

Still down on his knees, he waited without breathing. He did not make a sound.

The birds were still singing. His enemies must have moved off— but suddenly, the birds stopped singing. Someone was coming, even if he could not hear anything.

Robin Hood got down and put his ear to the ground. His acute hearing told him that someone was walking slowly, to his right, about thirty steps away.

Slowly, he raised his head. At first he saw nothing, but then he saw something moving among the trees beyond a row of bushes.

One shadow, then another. There were two men. They were dressed in black, and they walked one behind the other, cautious and attentive.

Robin shouted, "Stop there! Do not move or you're dead!" and he jumped to his feet, pulling back on his bow. The two men, taken by surprise, froze in their tracks.

Keeping them in range, Robin ordered, "Throw your weapons to the ground! Now!"

In a split second Ahmed and Abdul turned and, quick as lightning, a dagger and an arrow whistled by the outlaw's head.

In response, Robin shot his arrow and then jumped aside to hide behind a tree. But there was a brief shout after his shot, followed by a thud. As always, Robin Hood had not missed his target.

He shouted, "Surrender, or you will end up like your companion!" In response, an arrow planted itself in the tree. Robin looked at it. The arrow was black.

He shouted, "You cannot escape! Surrender!" The man fled.

Robin came out from behind the tree and moved forward slowly. In the bushes lay a man pierced by an arrow, and in his belt, he carried a long scimitar. It was Ahmed.

Only Abdul, then, still remained in the forest of Sherwood . . .

A DUEL WITH BOW AND ARROW

Robin hurried to follow the fugitive. He had to take advantage of that moment to pounce upon him.

It was necessary to act with great caution, however, because in the forest, the bow was more dangerous than the sword, thus it was riskier to follow than to flee. If he who was fleeing had a small lead, he could suddenly stop and take aim at his hunter. Robin had battled the sheriff's men this way many times.

For a while, Robin ran in the tracks that the archer left behind. Then he stopped, listened, and from the sound of the steps understood that the fugitive was going toward a large field bordered by the forest. If he reached the field, he would be able to lie in wait in the trees, then take aim and shoot Robin Hood, in the open field. So Robin left the trail and cut off in another direction. Meanwhile, Abdul continued in his desperate flight. It mattered little to him that his friend Ahmed was dead; what counted was saving his own life and not missing his mark. He ran as fast as possible, in order to be able to stop and shoot an arrow into his follower's heart. "I am more skilled than you, Robin Hood," the Saracen said to himself, continuing to flee, "and I will give you an unpleasant surprise!"

He passed a thicket, found himself in front of a brook, on the other side of which stood a field bordered on the rear by a forest. He walked into the brook, got out, and calling upon all his resources, began to cross the field. He would hide himself behind the first tree, and from there he would hit Robin Hood as he ran out into the open. "Like a rabbit!" he thought, "I will kill him like a rabbit!" Abdul ran faster. There were only fifty meters more to go, then forty, thirty, twenty meters, and then …

"Stop!" Robin Hood came out of the forest, bow in hand. By paths that only he knew, he had overcome the Saracen, and now he blocked the road. Abdul stopped with a suffocated curse. Robin, keeping him in sight, took several steps forward and said, "Drop your bow and follow me. You will be judged by all the men of the forest."

"I will not follow you!" replied Abdul defiantly. "But I am ready to do battle with you, to kill you outright as I killed your sentry." At these words, the outlaw felt his heart race. "All right, I accept your challenge."

Abdul responded, "So be it," and he took his bow; pulling an arrow from his quiver, he added, "When we are ready, you count. When you get to five, we shoot. Agreed?"

"Yes," answered Robin. The two men stood face to face, at exactly thirty paces apart.

Holding his bow ready, and keeping himself low, Robin began to count: "One … two …" Before he could say "three" Abdul raised his bow and shot his arrow. Robin, however, was faster. With a jump he dodged the treacherous arrow, pulled back on his bow, and let go of the cord. Abdul, hit in the heart, fell suddenly to the ground.

SIR WILLIAM'S POTATOES

Winter came, and it was harder than usual. The merry men of the forest found themselves without any money and little game to hunt.

Robin Hood said to them, "Friends, we cannot stay here wringing our hands and waiting for spring. Let's get ready; if the rich merchants don't come to us, we will go to them."

"What would you like to do, Robin?" asked Friar Tuck.

Robin responded, "You remember William of Limby, that fat, puffed-up man full of money who wanted to marry Edith? Well, I know that he has a warehouse filled with sacks of potatoes. He sells them at high prices. With this cold, though, there is nothing else to eat and the people are forced to buy them. What do you say? Shall we go pay him a visit?"

And so, the following evening, Robin Hood and his five most faithful friends, dressed as farmers, went down to Limby.

In the morning, they went to knock on the door of the rich Sir William's house. Each of them had a large sack on his back.

"Who are you, what do you want?" asked the merchant rudely.

Little John responded, "We are

selling these nice potatoes, sir."
"I am not interested in potatoes, I have plenty!" said Sir William.
"No? All right, we will go sell them to someone else!" said Little John, but the merchant called him back.
"Wait! How much are you selling the potatoes for?" asked Sir William.
"Twenty-five coins per sack."
"Are you crazy? I'll give you ten!"
"Fifteen," said Robin Hood.
William of Limby shook his head. "Twelve and no more!"
"All right, twelve. But we want the money now, not later."
"All right," said Sir William, "But first, I want to examine the goods."
The merchant looked in the sacks and saw that the potatoes were good. He calculated that by buying them for twelve coins and selling them for fifty coins, he would make a profit.

So he paid for them. The mock farmers thanked him and went to buy bread, cheese, and other foods; then they left the village.
That evening there was a feast under the Great Oak. Sir William of Limby, however, did not celebrate. He brought the potatoes he had bought to the warehouse and there he counted his sacks. "I had eighty, I bought six, so, I should have eighty-six . . . Ha ha! Those idiots! I paid twelve coins; they were worth thirty! I will sell them for fifty!"
He counted the sacks, but he only had eighty. Thinking he had made a mistake, he counted again: eighty. Only after he had counted the sacks ten times did he realize that he had bought his own potatoes: Robin Hood had stolen those six sacks the night before.

ROBIN HOOD'S REVENGE

A year passed, then another. All the sheriff's efforts to capture the merry men of the forest had been in vain, and the reward of three hundred gold coins had done little to aid him. Then one day, an old man dressed in rags, hunchbacked and limping, with a long straggly gray beard and mud-splattered hair, presented himself at the sheriff's castle. The guards did not want to let him pass, and he began to protest. He began shouting so loudly that the sheriff heard him. "Who is shouting so?" asked the sheriff.

"An old stinking man who wants to speak with you," said the guards.

"Well, let him through. If he has nothing interesting to say to me, beat him as he deserves," said Sir Maddock. When the old man was in front of him, the sheriff asked, "Well? What do you have to say to me?" The old man murmured, "I can bring you Robin Hood alive."

"What are you saying, old man? Are you crazy?" asked the sheriff.

"I tell you that I can bring him in. In exchange, naturally, I want three hundred coins."

The old man spoke with such a confident tone that Sir Maddock was surprised. He said, "I promise you will have them."

"You swear on your honor, on the honor of the king?"

"Of course!" replied the sheriff, annoyed. Then the old man raised his shoulders, took off his wig, took off the fake beard, and with a firm and mocking voice, said, "Give them to me, then. I bring you Robin Hood. For as you can see, Maddock, I am Robin Hood."

Aghast, Sir Maddock took several steps backward, and then with a strangled voice, shouted, "Guards! Guards!" But Robin was quick to throw the heavy chain that locked the door.

"Why call the guards? Didn't you swear on your honor to give me my reward? First pay me the three hundred coins, then have me arrested!" responded Robin.

"Are you fooling me?" asked Sir Maddock. Robin replied, "Not for a moment! I turned myself in, therefore I have a right to the reward. Out with the money!" The sheriff took a bag from a chest. "Here," he mumbled. Robin Hood took the bag, checked its contents, hung it from his belt, and said, "I took the bag, you take me."

Maddock hesitated, then put his hand on Robin's shoulder. "I arrest you! Now, give me back this bag!" He pulled the bag from Robin's belt, shouting, "Guards!" But as he turned his back, Robin jumped on him, grabbed the bag, and leapt onto the windowsill.

"You took the bag, Maddock, you didn't keep your promise!"

"And you," exclaimed the sheriff, "keep yours by escaping?"

"I promised that I would bring you Robin Hood, and I did. If you aren't able to keep him, too bad! Goodbye!" and with that, Robin Hood leapt from the sill.

The sheriff unlocked the door and shouted, "Get him! It's Robin Hood!" to the guards. They leaned out the window, but Robin had leapt into the moat. He swam to the bank, jumped onto a horse and rode away.

"Follow him!" ordered the sheriff. But no one could catch Robin Hood. He galloped to the well, lowered himself down, and left Nottingham by way of the secret passageway. His men were waiting for him at the edge of the forest. Triumphant, he showed them his rich booty.

THE END OF SIR MADDOCK

The order came again from London to capture the bandits of Sherwood Forest at all costs. Sir Maddock had twenty-one suits of armor prepared. The suits were brought out; he and twenty soldiers he had chosen put them on. At the head of this small army, Sir Maddock began his advance on the forest, until he ran into a group of outlaws.

The outlaws tried to defend themselves with their bows, but their arrows broke against the armor.

The news was brought to Robin by the lone survivor. There was great alarm. But Robin calmly said, "No, Sir Maddock will not be able to do anything."

"What will we do, Robin?" asked Friar Tuck. "If they come here with suits of armor, how will we defend ourselves? All we have are bows and arrows!"

"We will dig holes and pits and the armored men will fall into them."

And so they did. When Sir Maddock and his men made their attack on the clearing of the Great Oak, the ground swallowed many of them. Others, scared, retreated, but the sheriff, avoiding the pits, advanced furiously with his sword, and the outlaws had to flee.

Robin Hood undaunted as always, sword in hand, stayed to wait for his adversary.

Sir Maddock shouted, "Robin Hood, it's down to the two of us!"

"Yes, it is down to the two of us!"

The duel began, but every advance by Robin Hood was repelled by Sir Maddock's armor; he came forward without tiring, making his sword whirl and flash in front of him. "Robin Hood, this is the end!" Maddock exclaimed.

Robin Hood, warding off his attacks evenly, took a step backward and replied, "Don't be so sure, Maddock!" The sheriff, ever angrier, pressed in on Robin, who continued to draw back, going right, left, and finally finding himself up against a large oak tree.

"You are dead!" shouted Maddock as he stepped forward impetuously. Suddenly he disappeared into a deep well. The well was invisible in the tall grass; it opened up right in front of the oak tree.

Robin Hood had led Maddock to this very place with his retreat.

And that was the end of Sheriff Maddock.

THE YEARS GO BY

The years passed and many of Robin's friends disappeared, even the beautiful Marian and Edith, alas. They died quietly, one just a few days after the other, and they were laid to rest amid the flowers.

"What will we do now, Robin?" asked Alan, his face lined with tears.

Robin responded, "From what I have heard, soon King John will make a proclamation wherein he will spare all the outlaws, who will be able to live peacefully in their homes. Friends, I suggest that you leave Sherwood, and begin a new life."

"No, I will stay here with you, Robin!" exclaimed Scarlet.

Little John, then Friar Tuck, Alan, and Midge all shouted together, "We will stay with you, Robin!"

Thus, of the merry company of the forest, Robin's most faithful, courageous, and dearest friends remained. A book could not list all their adventures. But let us say that they were considered legendary characters. The minstrels, going from castle to castle, sang of their many deeds.

From the beginning, King John had forbidden songs, stories, and poetry about the merry men of Sherwood.

Later on, he changed his mind, and here is how it happened. One day the king was at the table with his guests, when a lady asked a minstrel to tell a story of adventure and love. "I will tell, then," said the minstrel, "of how a young man named Alan Dale came to marry his beloved." Playing smooth strokes on his harp, he sang the story of Edith, who had to marry William of Limby, although she loved Alan. He told of how the church was already adorned with flowers and full of guests; he even described the pale face and teary eyes of the maiden. He did it so well that the king exclaimed, "By Jove! I hope that someone came and put a stop to this unhappy wedding!"

"Yes, Sire, someone did. It was a minstrel, who instead of playing his harp played his horn, and a group of outlaws ran from the forest into the church, scaring everyone there." King John laughed. "And then what happened?" he asked.

"The minstrel ordered the priest to marry the girl and her true beloved, and it was done," was the reply.

"What was the minstrel's name?" asked the king. "Robin Hood," said the minstrel.

The king was silent.

THE ABBEY AT KIRKLEYS

One day, Robin Hood was overcome with a feeling of sickness.

He drank some water from a spring and it seemed bitter to him; he ate an apple and it seemed even more bitter. He said then, "Friends, I think I have to go to a doctor."

"You should go to Nottingham or Sheffield for a doctor, but they are full of guards and soldiers these days," observed Midge, who had been in the city not long before.

Robin Hood said, "I will go then to the abbess of Kirkleys, who is my good cousin, and is practiced in medicine."

Scarlet said, "Go ahead to Kirkleys, Robin, but not alone. We will come with you, and if anything happens, we will all confront it."

"What could happen?" asked Robin. "One never knows, when women are involved," observed Friar Tuck. Everyone laughed, and Robin said, "I will go to Kirkleys alone, friends, and I will go unarmed." Little John protested, "No, no. I will come with you and if you do not want to carry a bow, I will carry it for you." So it was decided and the two set off. It was the first time, after many years, that Robin Hood had been through the forest without a bow, and it did not please Little John so, after a while, he said, "Robin, it would be better if you took the bow." So that his words would not be taken as disobedience or lack of respect, he added, "I want to challenge you to a contest along the way."

Robin Hood could not refuse. The road was traveled happily anyway, but at a point where the trees divided, the two saw, beside a hut, an old woman who was bent over a board, washing her clothes.

"How sad that woman is," whispered Little John. Robin Hood shrugged his shoulders and continued down the road. Hearing the sound of steps, the woman turned and asked, "Are you Robin Hood?"

"Yes," was the response. The old woman, grinding her teeth, mumbled some curse. Surprised, Robin asked, "Why do you curse me?" The woman returned to her work without answering, and the two continued on, disturbed by the mysterious encounter. Little John felt a cold shiver pass down his spine. It seemed to him that there was some sign of destiny in those curses. The two continued down the road, arriving at noon the next day. The abbey was pretty, the grounds were beautiful, but despite this, an air of sadness and misfortune reigned. Little John stopped and whispered, "Robin, I don't like this place. It brings bad luck, I am sure. Let's go."

"Go on, Little John, are you afraid of the good sisters? Here," and so saying, Robin Hood gave him his bow, "one cannot enter a place of peace armed. Wait for me here. I won't be long."

"Robin ... " began Little John, but the other didn't hear. Robin Hood knocked on the abbey door; an old nun came to the door and asked, "Who is it?"

"I am Robin, the abbess's cousin. I would like to speak with her."

"Come in," said the nun.

THE ABBESS'S BETRAYAL

In the time that had passed, an inexplicable and strong unrest had overcome the outlaws who had stayed under the Great Oak, so much so that Friar Tuck, Alan, and Midge set out for the abbey.

Meanwhile, the abbess stood before Robin. She was a withered and thin woman, with a bony face and small, diffident eyes. As soon as she saw Robin she thought, "He is my cousin, yes, but he is also a bandit; if I take this man, dead or alive, to the Sheriff of Nottingham and the king, I will certainly reap a great reward." This nasty thought was not reflected in her face, and smiling, she said, "Ah, Robin, welcome! I am happy to see you! Why have you left your kingdom of Sherwood to come here?" "Good cousin, I do not feel very well, and I would like you to tell me what medicine to take," answered Robin.

The abbess asked him some questions and finally concluded, "With a bloodletting, cousin, you will be fine right away. Come into this room and wait for me," she added.

"First, take this," he told her, giving her twenty gold coins.

The abbess left, and after a little while she returned to the room and ordered, "Lie down on that cot, and give me your arm."

Robin trustingly obeyed. The abbess, practiced in bloodletting, cut a vein to allow the blood to flow out. However, she did it so that the wound was very deep and would not heal quickly.

As the blood began to flow, she said with a false smile, "Now, close your eyes and sleep peacefully, cousin. I will take care of everything. I will wake you in a little while."

As soon as she saw Robin was sleeping, she left the room.

"I have won! The king will be grateful, and he will make me abbess of an important abbey!" she thought as she went off.

Time passed slowly and the blood flowed ever more slowly.

Robin Hood was not asleep, only drowsy. At first, the bloodletting proved to be a relief, but then he began to feel very weak. He made himself sit up, and he looked at the wound.

He saw that by now little blood flowed out of it. Robin Hood realized immediately that he had been betrayed by his cousin.

He tried to alert Little John.

Robin Hood had gone into the abbey unarmed, but he still had his horn in his belt.

He brought it to his mouth, and with a supreme effort blew into it with his last remaining breath.

ROBIN HOOD'S LAST ARROW

Little John, who was waiting seated under a tree, heard the horn, and jumped to his feet with his heart racing. This was not a call that he had heard, but a plea. Robin was in danger. The large man hurried to the abbey and knocked loudly. He waited few minutes, and with a kick, knocked down the door.

He didn't see anyone. Hearing the horn, the terrified abbess hid herself in the most secret corner of the convent, and with her, her nuns.

"Robin Hood!" Little John began to call, "Where are you?" He ran through the convent, looking ever more frantically into each room. Finally, he found Robin stretched out on the cot. He understood the betrayal immediately and that there was nothing that could be done.

"Robin!" he cried.

Hearing his friend's voice, Robin Hood turned his pale face, managed a smile, and murmured, "Little John, you have come ... my end is near."

Trying not to cry, Little John knelt down. "Be a good friend to the others," said Robin Hood.

"We will always be friends in your name, Robin!" answered Little John.

"Little John, keep my bow, will you promise?" Kneeling beside the cot, Little John said with a sigh, "Yes ... but now I have one last favor to ask of you, Robin."

"What do you want?" asked Robin.

"Let me set fire to this abbey and to all the nuns who live here."

A tired smile passed over Robin Hood's bloodless lips, and he answered, "Little John, you know that I have never raised a hand against a woman, or against a man who was in the company of a woman. You will do nothing. Give me my bow and an arrow."

Just then, they heard footsteps, and voices calling, "Robin Hood! Robin Hood!" Little John went to the threshold and there he saw Friar Tuck, Midge, Scarlet, and Alan.

"In here, friends!" he said.

Shortly, the surviving members of the great band of Sherwood were all on their knees before their leader.

"Here is your bow," said Little John. Robin Hood whispered, "Help me sit up and give me an arrow."

This done, Robin cocked the arrow, saying, "Bury me where you find this arrow." He aimed his bow out of the window, pulled back on it, and let go. The arrow sailed away, and with it the infallible archer's life also vanished.

Carrying the body of their leader, the outlaws left the cursed abbey. They looked for Robin Hood's arrow and finally found it planted in an ancient oak tree.

They dug a deep hole under the tree and this became Robin Hood's grave.

THE END

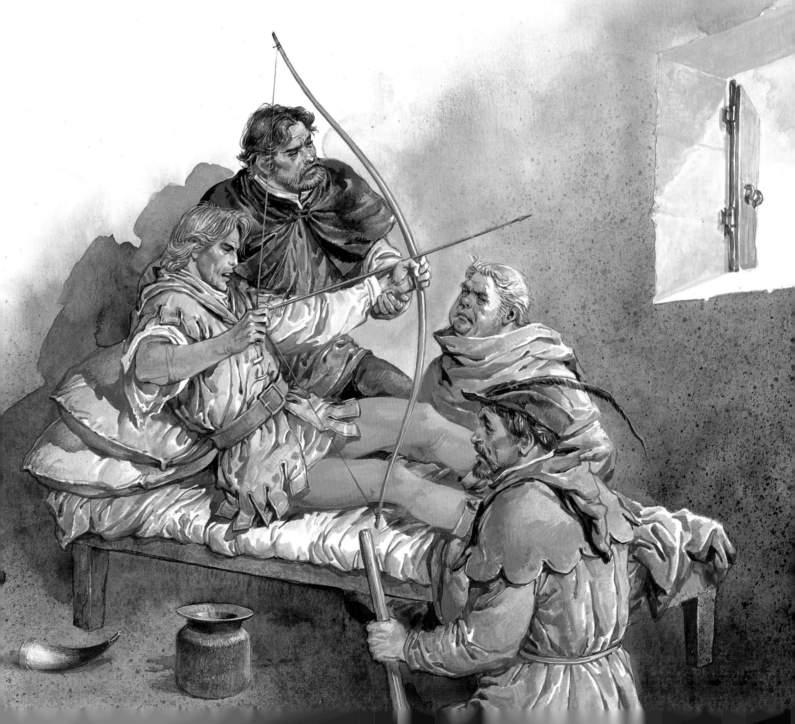